DANIEL TIGER'S NEIGHBORHOOD

Daniel Plays in a Gentle Way

Adapted by Alexandra Cassel Schwartz
Based on the screenplay "Daniel's Obstacle Course" written by Jill Cozza-Turner
Poses and layouts by Jason Fruchter

Simon Spotlight
New York   London   Toronto   Sydney   New Delhi

SIMON SPOTLIGHT
An imprint of Simon & Schuster Children's Publishing Division
1230 Avenue of the Americas, New York, New York 10020
This Simon Spotlight paperback edition May 2020
© 2020 The Fred Rogers Company
SIMON SPOTLIGHT and colophon are registered trademarks of Simon & Schuster, Inc.
For information about special discounts for bulk purchases, please contact Simon & Schuster
Special Sales at 1-866-506-1949 or business@simonandschuster.com.
Manufactured in the United States of America 0320 LAK
10 9 8 7 6 5 4 3 2 1
ISBN 978-1-5344-6448-3 (pbk)
ISBN 978-1-5344-6449-0 (eBook)

Then he hopped across the block bridge!

Then Daniel snuck around the basket mountains.

And finally, Daniel jumped into the soft pillow clouds!

"Come on, Margaret!" Daniel said. He wanted to play with his sister on the obstacle course.

They crawled through the cushion tunnel together.

"Faster, Margaret, faster!" Daniel shouted. Daniel tugged on Margaret's arm to help her over the block bridge, but Margaret couldn't go as fast as her big brother.

Margaret fell on the block bridge and started to cry.
"I'm sorry, Margaret," said Daniel. "We can try again. Come on!"
Daniel tugged on his sister's arm again, but she didn't want to
play on the obstacle course anymore. She was upset.

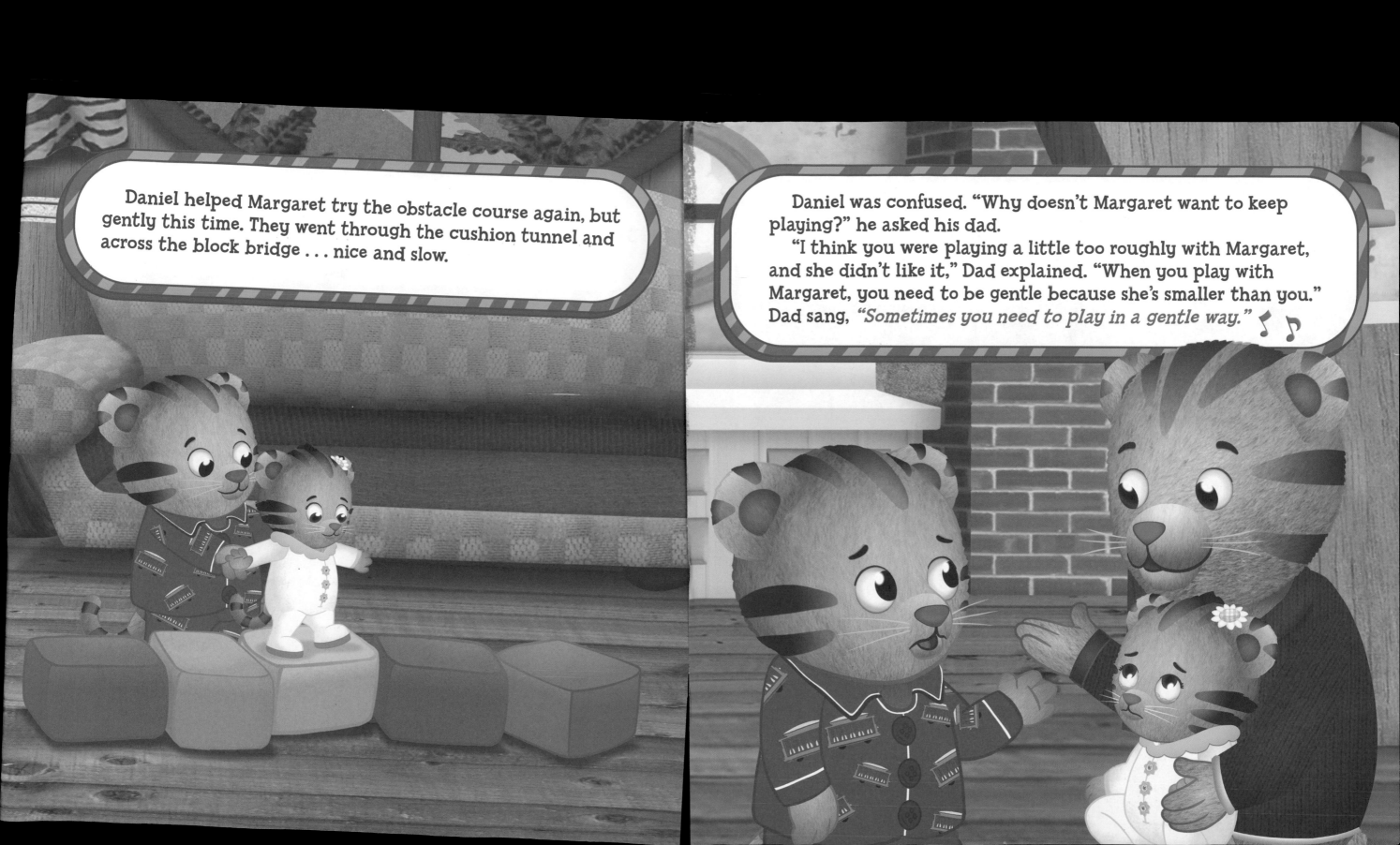

Daniel helped Margaret try the obstacle course again, but gently this time. They went through the cushion tunnel and across the block bridge . . . nice and slow.

Daniel was confused. "Why doesn't Margaret want to keep playing?" he asked his dad.

"I think you were playing a little too roughly with Margaret, and she didn't like it," Dad explained. "When you play with Margaret, you need to be gentle because she's smaller than you." Dad sang, *"Sometimes you need to play in a gentle way."*

Finally, Daniel and Margaret reached the soft pillow clouds. "So soft and fluffy!" Daniel said. They giggled together. Margaret liked playing gently with her big brother.

"We did it!" Daniel cheered loudly. "Let's play again! Go, Margaret, go!"

Daniel's voice got louder and louder. Margaret started to cry.

Daniel was being too loud, and his baby sister didn't like that. *"Sometimes you need to play in a gentle way,"* Daniel sang.

He began to talk quietly, and that made Margaret smile.

"I have an idea," said Daniel. "Maybe Trolley and Tigey want to try the obstacle course this time."
He pushed his trolley gently through the cushion tunnel.

Then Daniel gave his sister a turn pushing his trolley too. But when Margaret got excited, she banged the trolley against the floor.

"No, Margaret!" Daniel said. "You're being too rough with the trolley." Daniel was upset.

Now Daniel and Margaret both knew how to play in a gentle way.